MW01689495

Blitz® Ultimate Cartooning Book

By
Bruce Blitz

RUNNING PRESS
PHILADELPHIA • LONDON

© 2004 BY BRUCE BLITZ

ALL RIGHTS RESERVED UNDER THE PAN-AMERICAN
AND INTERNATIONAL COPYRIGHT CONVENTIONS

PRINTED IN CHINA

THIS BOOK MAY NOT BE REPRODUCED IN WHOLE OR IN PART, IN ANY FORM OR BY ANY MEANS, ELECTRONIC OR MECHANICAL, INCLUDING PHOTOCOPYING, RECORDING, OR BY ANY INFORMATION STORAGE AND RETRIEVAL SYSTEM NOW KNOWN OR HEREAFTER INVENTED, WITHOUT WRITTEN PERMISSION FROM THE PUBLISHER.

9 8 7 6 5 4 3 2 1

DIGIT ON THE RIGHT INDICATES THE NUMBER OF THIS PRINTING

LIBRARY OF CONGRESS CONTROL NUMBER 2003115261

ISBN 0-7624-1928-8

COVER AND INTERIOR DESIGN BY MATTHEW GOODMAN
EDITED BY GREG JONES
TYPOGRAPHY: MEANWHILE, AND SMASH

THIS BOOK MAY BE ORDERED BY MAIL FROM THE PUBLISHER.
PLEASE INCLUDE $2.50 FOR POSTAGE AND HANDLING.
BUT TRY YOUR BOOKSTORE FIRST!

PUBLISHED BY RUNNING PRESS KIDS, AN IMPRINT OF
RUNNING PRESS BOOK PUBLISHERS
125 SOUTH TWENTY-SECOND STREET
PHILADELPHIA, PENNSYLVANIA 19103-4399

VISIT US ON THE WEB!
WWW.RUNNINGPRESS.COM

Contents

Re-Tooner™ Boards

WELCOME! I'M BRUCE BLITZ
...AND WE'RE BROADCASTING LIVE TO SHOW HOW THE BLITZ RE-TOONER™ HAS CHANGED PEOPLE'S LIVES!
CLICK CLICK
CLICK
NOW THAT I AM A CARTOONIST, THE PAPARAZZI FOLLOW ME EVERYWHERE!
CLICK CLICK CLICK
CLICK
HOW ABOUT YOU, MISS?
THE BLITZ RE-TOONER™ MADE ME WHAT I AM TODAY!
MEANWHILE...DOWNTOWN
THANKS TO THE BLITZ RE-TOONER™, I ALWAYS GET THE BEST TABLE!
YOUR TABLE IS READY, SIR.
HEY... WE'VE BEEN WAITING 2 HOURS!
BE QUIET! HE'S A CARTOONIST!
MENU
NOW IT'S YOUR TURN TO BECOME A GREAT CARTOONIST. LET'S GO!

Introduction

IT'S ALL ABOUT COMMUNICATION . . . AND PICTURES COMMUNICATE BETTER THAN WORDS! BEFORE CAMERAS WERE INVENTED, PICTURES HAD TO BE HAND DRAWN. THIS GOES BACK TO THE WALLS OF CAVES.

THESE DRAWINGS WERE NOT VERY DETAILED, EITHER. THEY DIDN'T HAVE TO BE. ALL IT TOOK WAS A FEW LINES HERE AND THERE TO COMMUNICATE AN IDEA. YOU COULD SAY THAT THESE DRAWINGS WERE THE FIRST CARTOONS! THAT'S RIGHT, BECAUSE CARTOONING IS AN "ABBREVIATED" FORM OF ART. YOU CAN SAY A LOT WITHOUT TOO MUCH DETAIL.

CARTOONING IS USED TODAY IN THE SAME WAY. CARTOONS ARE USED TO: COMMUNICATE IDEAS, TELL JOKES AND STORIES . . .

. . . AND EVEN INSTRUCT. THEY REMIND US NOT TO TAKE OURSELVES TOO SERIOUSLY, LIKE THIS CARICATURE HERE.

MY LOVE FOR CARTOONING BEGAN LIKE MOST PEOPLE'S: BY LAUGHING AT THE COMICS IN THE NEWSPAPER, READING COMIC BOOKS, AND WATCHING ANIMATED CARTOONS ON TELEVISION.

Me at nine years old

I REMEMBER ONCE AT A YOUNG AGE, SEEING A HUGE, BRIGHT, COLORFULLY PAINTED MENU SIGN IN A SANDWICH SHOP THAT HAD HUMOROUS DRAWINGS OF CARTOON CHARACTERS IN VARIOUS POSES THROUGHOUT THE SIGN—EATING AND DRINKING SANDWICHES AND MILKSHAKES. IT REALLY COMMANDED ATTENTION, AND I WAS HOOKED. I WAS HOOKED ON CARTOONING. ALL I CAN REMEMBER IS SAYING TO MYSELF THAT I WANTED TO LEARN HOW TO CREATE IMAGES LIKE THAT, TOO.

THE QUESTION I AM MOST OFTEN ASKED IS: ARE YOU BORN WITH ART TALENT, OR CAN THE ABILITY TO DRAW BE LEARNED? THE ANSWER IS: BOTH. SOME PEOPLE MAY HAVE MORE NATURAL ABILITY THAN OTHERS, BUT I AM CONVINCED THIS BOOK—AND THE BLITZ® RE-TOONER™—WILL MAKE YOU A BETTER CARTOONIST FROM WHATEVER POINT YOU START. SO LET'S DRAW CARTOONS!

What's in the Kit?

How to Use Your Blitz® Re-Tooner™

1. SELECT ONE OF YOUR FIFTY RE-TOONER™ BOARDS.

2. INSERT A PLASTIC SHEET INTO THE RE-TOONER™ STAND, THEN SLIDE THE RE-TOONER™ BOARD UNDER IT.

3. USE YOUR DRY ERASE MARKER TO FILL IN ANY MISSING AREAS, AND DO WHAT EACH BOARD TELLS YOU TO DO.

4. USE YOUR WIPE-OFF CLOTH TO WIPE OFF WHAT YOU'VE DONE AND TRY SOMETHING NEW!

Remember!

DON'T DRAW DIRECTLY ON ANY RE-TOONER™ BOARD! ALWAYS SLIDE IT INTO THE RE-TOONER™ STAND UNDER THE SEE-THROUGH SHEETS. THIS WAY, YOU CAN ERASE WHAT YOU'VE DONE, AND RE-TOON OVER AND OVER! WHAT A GREAT WAY TO LEARN! ALSO, ONLY USE YOUR SPECIAL DRY ERASE MARKERS ON YOUR RE-TOONER™ SEE-THROUGH SHEETS—ANY OTHER MARKER OR PEN MAY LEAVE A PERMANENT MARK.

Cartoon Heads

LET'S BEGIN WITH SOME BASIC SHAPES.

Oval

1. LET'S START BY DRAWING TWO GUIDE-LINES IN EACH SHAPE

2. THEN ADD TWO EYES, EYEBROWS, AND A NOSE

3. DRAW IN THE MOUTH, EARS, AND HAIR

4. FINALLY, "INK IN" OVER THE PENCIL TO CREATE ONE DEFINITE CLEAN BLACK LINE

Rectangle

More Variations

HERE WE HAVE SOME DIFFERENT BEGINNING SHAPES TO CREATE DIFFERENT CARTOON CHARACTERS.

Upside-down teardrop

Triangle

Upside-down triangle

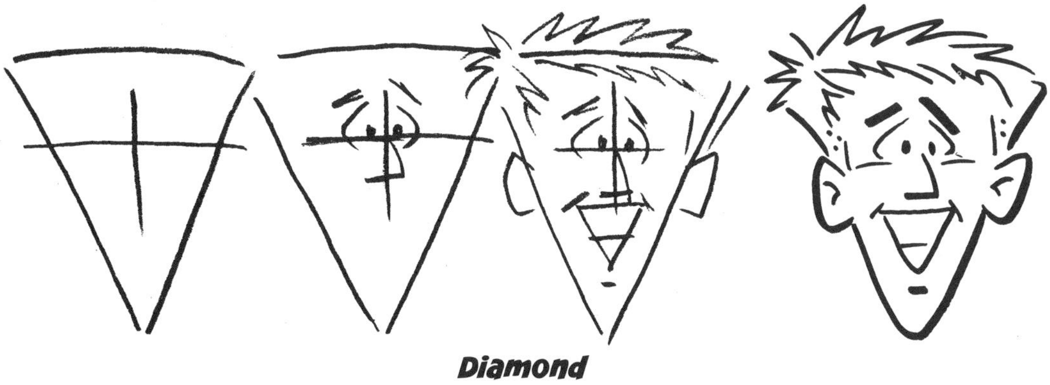

Diamond

More Cartoon Heads

LET'S TAKE THIS A BIT FURTHER. BY PLAYING AROUND WITH BASIC FACIAL FEATURES—THAT IS, CHANGING THE WAY THEY ARE DRAWN, THEIR SIZES, AND THEIR PLACEMENT—WE CAN COME UP WITH A LOT MORE FACES.

Hairstyles & Head Shapes

Fruit Heads

HEAD-SHAPED INSPIRATION IS EVERYWHERE!

Carrot

Onion

Turnip

Pineapple

Banana

Features

Eyes

Noses

Mouths

Eyes Looking Around

BY REPOSITIONING THE PUPILS, YOU CAN GET EYES TO LOOK EVERYWHERE.

Side-View Heads

Go to Re-Tooner™

BOARDS #1, #2, AND #3 AND EXPERIMENT WITH CREATING TONS OF CARTOON HEADS; THEN JOIN ME ON THE NEXT PAGE.

Turning Heads

UP UNTIL NOW, THE HEADS WE'VE BEEN DRAWING HAVE BEEN FACING US. NOW, WE WILL DRAW FACES THAT LOOK IN DIFFERENT DIRECTIONS. YOU CAN DO THIS BY THINKING OF THE SHAPE AS A THREE-DIMENSIONAL OBJECT—SUCH AS AN EGG— AND WRAP YOUR GUIDELINES "AROUND" IT. THEN, WHEN YOU ADD YOUR FEATURES WHERE THE GUIDELINES ARE, YOUR FACES CAN FACE ALL OVER THE PLACE!

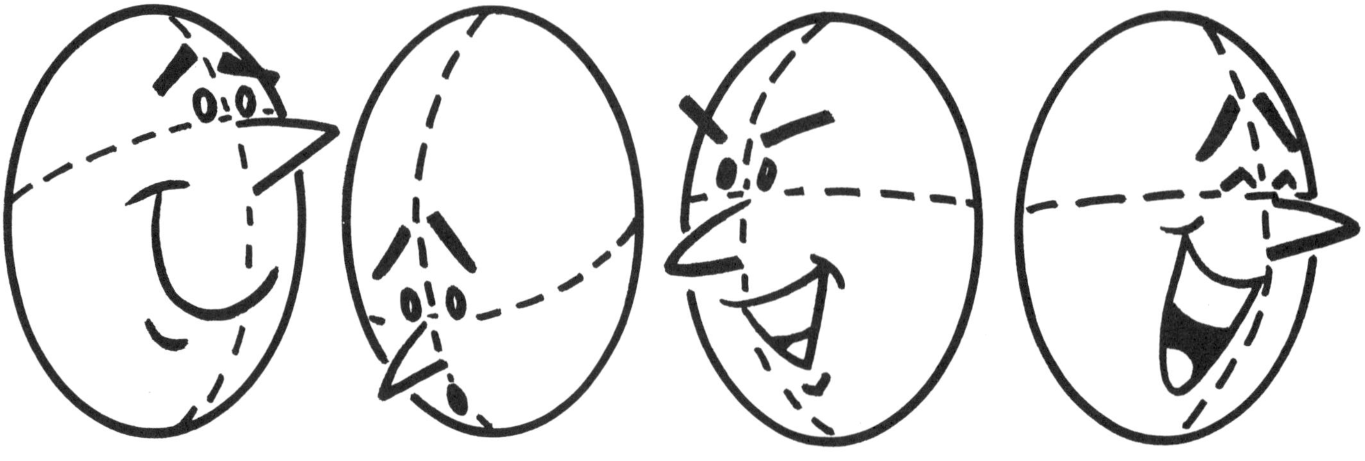

Up *Down* *Left* *Right*

Jar *Football* *Ice-cream cone* *Teardrop*

HERE'S WHY BEING ABLE TO DRAW CARTOONS FACING IN DIFFERENT DIRECTIONS COMES IN HANDY. IT MAKES YOUR CHARACTERS APPEAR MORE REAL AND NOT WOODEN.

Wrong

Right

YOU CAN'T ALWAYS HAVE YOUR CHARACTERS FACE FRONT OR SIDE. SOMETIMES THEY HAVE TO BE FACING SOMEWHERE BETWEEN THE TWO.

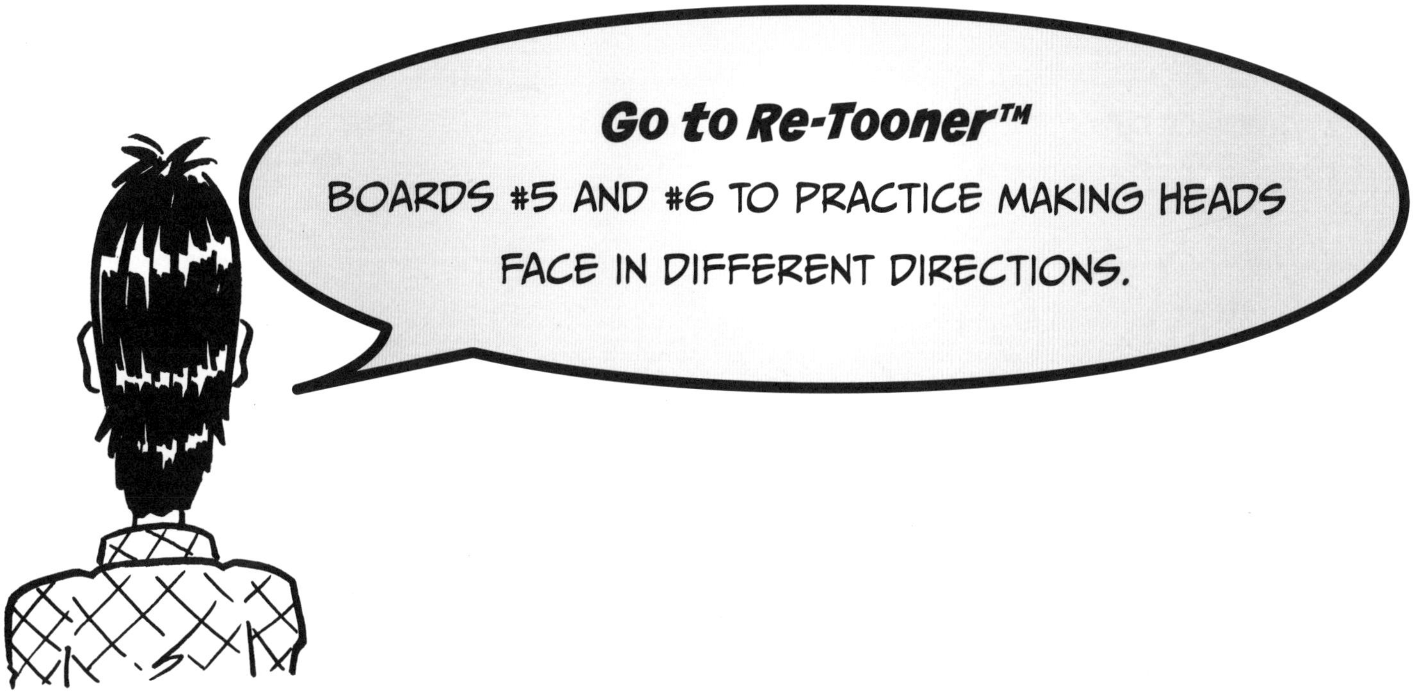

Facial Accessories

Beards & Mustaches

Goatee & Thin Mustache

White Goatee and Droopy Mustache

Fancy Handlebar Mustache

This guy looks like a strong man in the circus.

Curly Beard

Hey, its Santa!

Glasses

HERE ARE SEVERAL WAYS TO DRAW EYEGLASSES.

Hats

TRY SOME OF THESE HATS ON FOR SIZE.
THEN TRY CREATING YOUR OWN FUNNY HATS AND GLASSES!

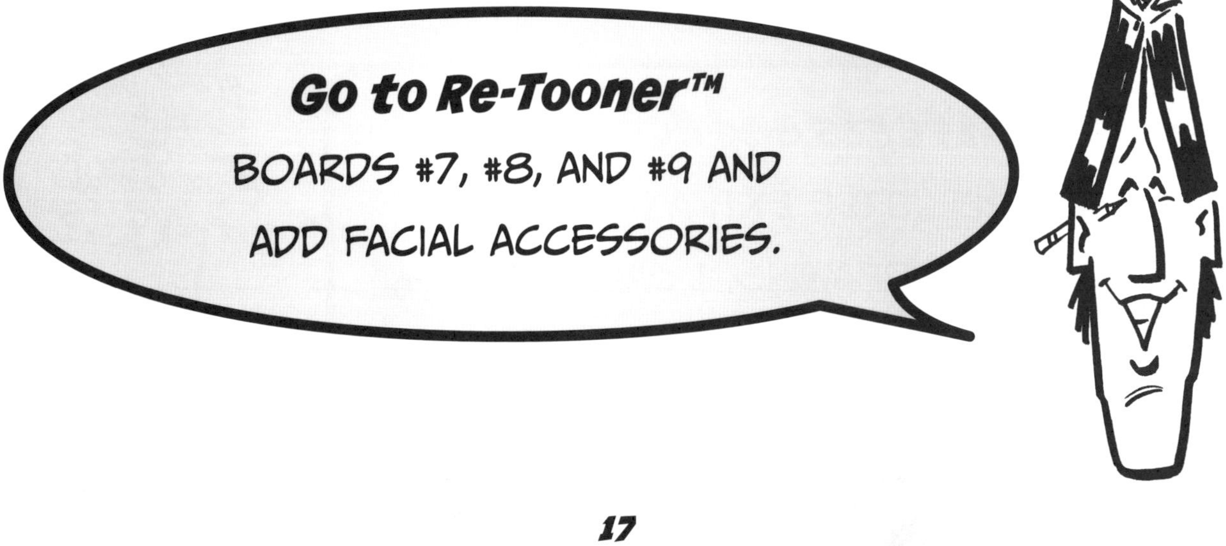

Expressions

YOUR CHARACTERS ARE YOUR ACTORS, AND YOUR PAPER IS YOUR FILM. STUDY THE EMOTIONS BELOW. JUST LIKE YOU CAN'T ALWAYS HAVE YOUR CHARACTERS FACING ONE DIRECTION, YOU CAN'T HAVE YOUR CHARACTERS HAVING ONE EXPRESSION. NOTE HOW ONE EXPRESSION CAN FIT SEVERAL EMOTIONS. IT ALL DEPENDS ON WHAT ELSE IS HAPPENING IN THE SCENE.

Yelling or Angry

Snob

IF YOU CHANGE THE SOUND EFFECT "HMPH!" TO "ZZZZ," SHE WOULD LOOK LIKE SHE'S ASLEEP.

Dazed or Sleepy

Sobbing or Brokenhearted

Thinking or Suspicious

Cartoon Effects and Accessories

NOTICE THE LITTLE EXTRA DOODLES AROUND EACH DRAWING, I CALL THESE "CARTOON EFFECTS AND ACCESSORIES." THEY HELP YOUR CARTOONS COME ALIVE!

Laughing

Coy or Embarrassed

Crying

Scared

Nervous

Sleeping

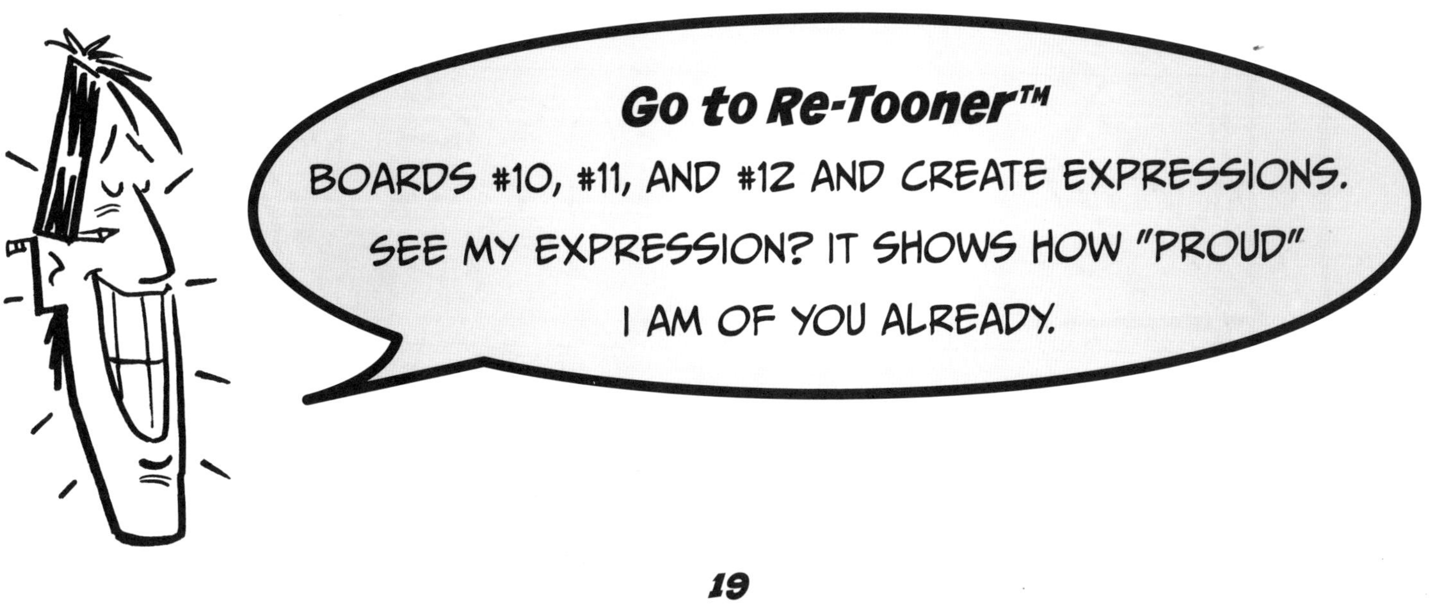

It's Time to Act!

HERE ARE A FEW SCENES THAT HAVE TWO CHARACTERS IN EACH. NOTICE HOW THEIR FACIAL EXPRESSIONS MATCH THE ACTION AND HOW THEY REACT TO EACH OTHER.

Angry **Sad**

Happy **Scared**

Smug *Frustrated*

Go to Re-Tooner™

BOARDS #13, #14, AND #15 AND FILL IN THE APPROPRIATE FACIAL EXPRESSION TO HAVE YOUR CHARACTERS BECOME AWARD-WINNING ACTORS TO FIT THE SCENE.

Inanimate Objects Come to Life

ANYTHING IS POSSIBLE IN THE WORLD OF CARTOONING! TAKE THESE WELL-KNOWN OBJECTS, FOR EXAMPLE. IN THESE CARTOONS, THEY HAVE BEEN GIVEN LIFE BY SIMPLY ADDING FACIAL FEATURES AND EXPRESSIONS TO REFLECT A PERSONALITY. THIS WORKS ESPECIALLY WELL WHEN YOU INCORPORATE EXPRESSIONS BASED ON WHAT THE OBJECT IS USED FOR.

Cell phone

THINK ABOUT WHAT THE OBJECT DOES IN ORDER TO COME UP WITH IDEAS FOR THEM.

Umbrella (HE LOVES THE RAIN)

A ***Washer and Dryer*** FALL IN LOVE

Lamp

THESE EXAMPLES COULD BE USED FOR ADVERTISING CARTOONS.

THESE GUYS COULD BE USED FOR A SIGN.

THIS ***shopping cart*** COULD BE USED FOR A SUPERMARKET AD.

Cartoon Bodies

THERE ISN'T ANY ONE BODY PROPORTION USED TO CREATE CARTOON CHARACTERS. IT ALL DEPENDS ON WHAT TYPE OF CHARACTER YOU ARE CREATING, YOUR STYLE OF CARTOONING, AND MOST IMPORTANTLY, THE SHAPE YOU BEGIN WITH.

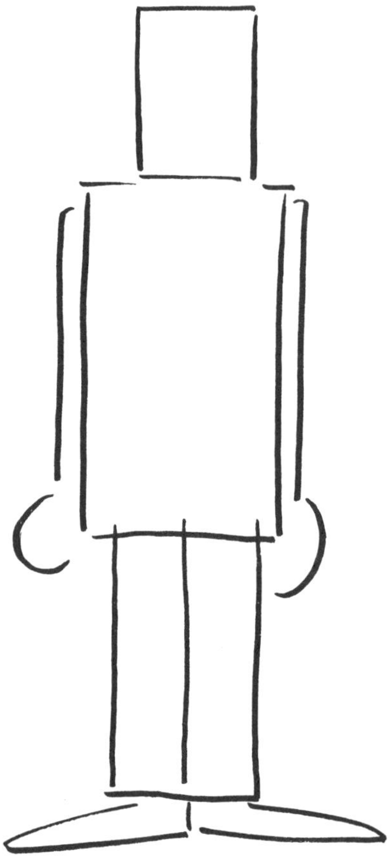

SQUARES, RECTANGLES, AND SHAPES FOR THE HANDS AND FEET ARE USED TO CREATE THIS ***businessman.***

A DIAMOND SHAPE . . .

. . . IS USED TO CREATE THIS ***tourist.***

REMEMBER CHANGING THE SHAPES YOU USED TO CREATE DIFFERENT CARTOON HEADS?
WELL, THE SAME GOES FOR CREATING DIFFERENT CARTOON BODIES.

OVAL FOR HEAD

TRIANGLE FOR TORSO

RECTANGLE FOR LEGS

AN ELONGATED TRIANGLE SIDE VIEW

TURN THE TRIANGLE UPSIDE-DOWN TO CREATE THIS SUPERHERO TYPE,

"Practice Man."

More Shapes & Characters

A LARGE OVAL . . .

. . . CREATED THIS WOMAN. NOTICE HOW THE DAINTY FEET, IN CONTRAST TO THE BODY, ADD AN EXTRA ELEMENT OF HUMOR.

MEDIUM-SIZED OVAL

ELONGATED OVAL

BY SQUEEZING THIS OVAL IN THE MIDDLE, WE CAN CONSTRUCT THIS WOMAN CHARACTER.

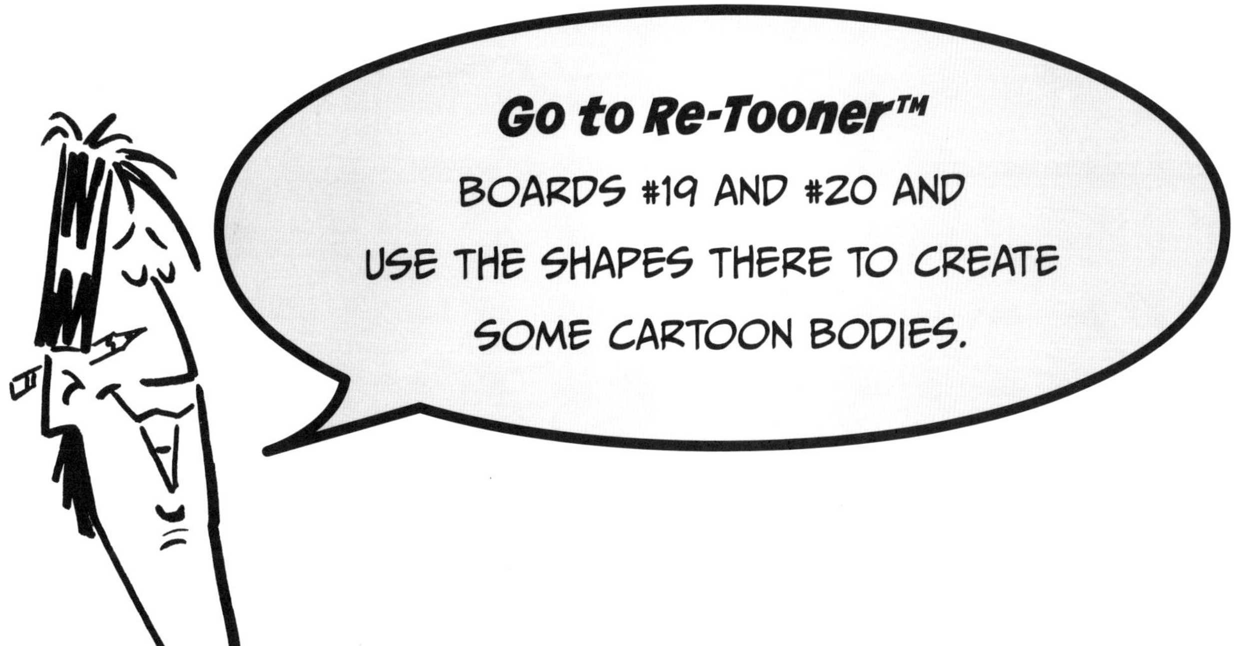
Go to Re-Tooner™
BOARDS #19 AND #20 AND USE THE SHAPES THERE TO CREATE SOME CARTOON BODIES.

Hands

IT'S BEST TO DRAW THEM SIMPLE.

Basic construction

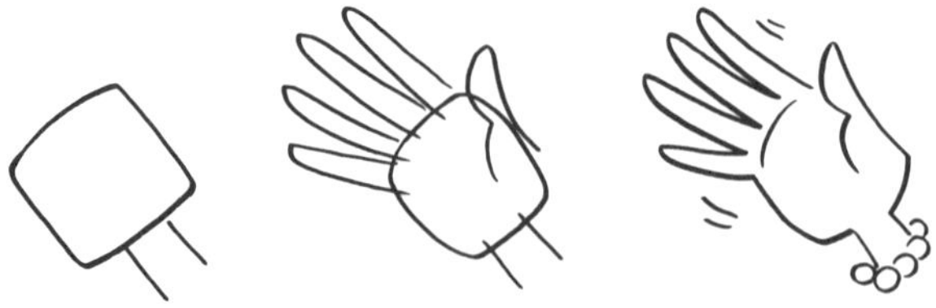

Womans Hands

Mens Hands

HANDS ARE EXPRESSIVE, ESPECIALLY WHEN YOU USE "CARTOON EFFECTS" AS SEEN HERE.

Waving

Halt

Peace

Snapping to the music

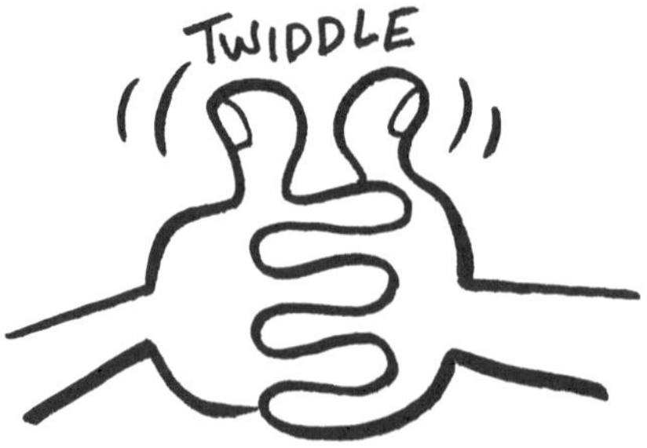

Impatience or bored

Encouragement

Leading a band

Accusing

Praying

Hold on!!

HANDS ARE ALSO USED TO HOLD THINGS.

Handshake

Wrapped around a soda can

Pencil

Book

Handle (palm facing in)

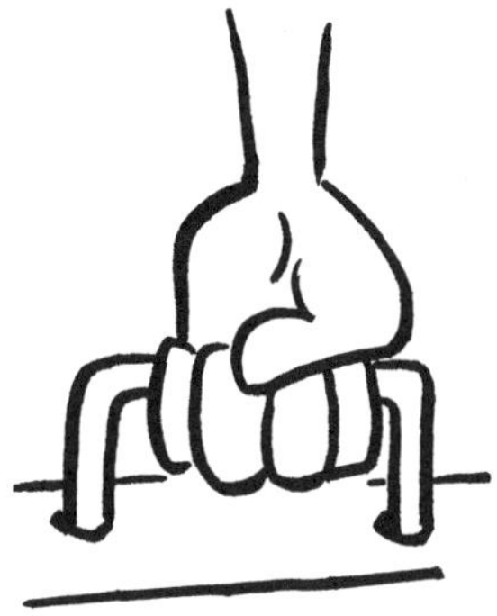

Handle (palm facing out)

Meet the Feet!

FEET CAN ADD A HUMOROUS ELEMENT TO YOUR DRAWINGS.

Basic construction

WHEN DRAWING A FOOT, DON'T FORGET TO DRAW THE HEEL.
IT HELPS TO ADD BALANCE TO YOUR CHARACTER.

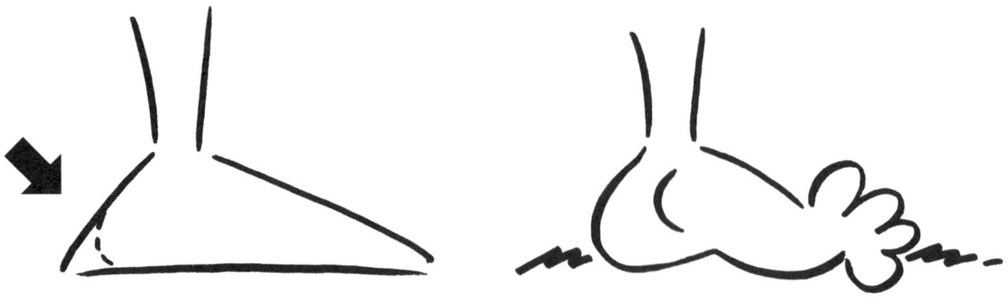

"Tootsies" from
THE BOTTOM

Loafers

Tap shoes

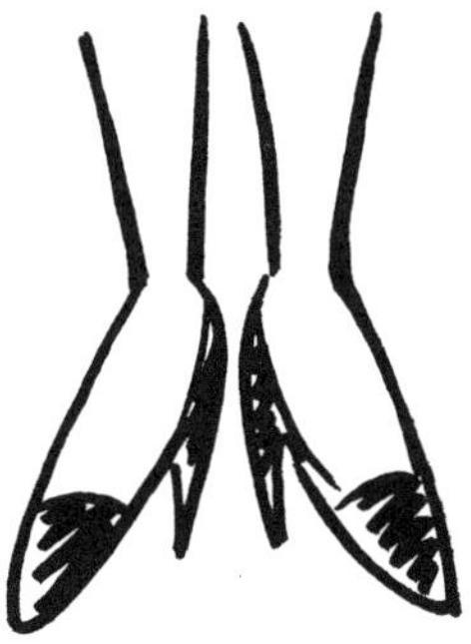

High heels

Plain lace-up shoes

Sandals

In-liners

Shoes in silhouette

Cast

Yipes Types

THESE ARE THE CHARACTERS THAT PLAY THE PARTS IN YOUR CARTOON WORLD. APPROPRIATE CLOTHING IS IMPORTANT IN DETERMINING HOW WELL THEY ACTUALLY LOOK LIKE WHO THEY ARE.

Doorman

Punk rocker

Fancy chef

Teacher or mom

Boss

A ***basketball player*** AND HIS ***slick manager***

A fast-talking lawyer or a game-show host

An absentminded professor or a scientist

A rich woman

Pirate

Cowboy

Surgeon

Granny

Football coach
or tough guy
(you decide)

Sumo wrestler

Head waiter

Glamorous movie star

Blitz® Tip:

PRACTICE IS THE MOTHER OF SUCCESS!

Go to Re-Tooner™

BOARDS #25, #26, AND #27 AND CREATE SOME CARTOON TYPES.

Cartoonist type

You've Got to be KID-ding

NOTICE HOW THE FEATURES ARE PLACED DOWN LOWER ON
THE HEAD SHAPE THAN WHEN DRAWING OLDER CHARACTERS.

Oh Baby

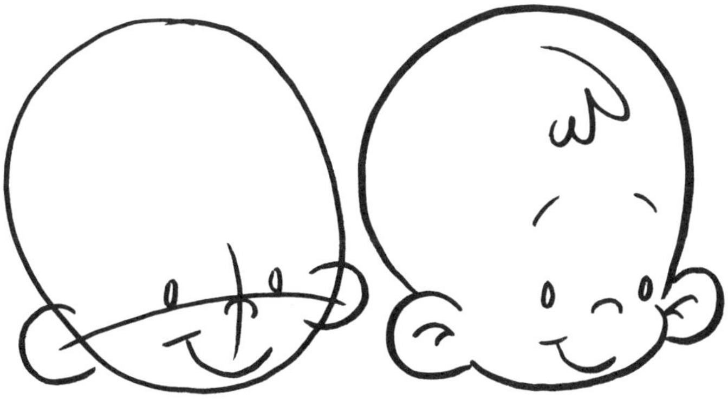

THE FEATURES ARE PLACED EVEN LOWER WHEN DRAWING BABIES. . .

. . . AND THE HEAD MAKES UP TWO-THIRDS OF THE FIGURE.

Chin Trick

JUST BY DRAWING THE CHIN LINE LOWER OR HIGHER, YOUR CHARACTERS WILL LOOK DIFFERENT AGES.

Three years old

Eight years old

Twelve years old

YOU CAN ADD A FEW YEARS TO YOUR CHARACTERS BY SIMPLY LENGTHENING THEIR LEGS.

TRY THIS BASEBALL POSE! I THINK HE'S GOING TO HIT A HOMER, TOO.

Blitz® Tip:

TELLING YOURSELF YOU CAN IS GOOD. SHOWING YOURSELF YOU CAN IS BETTER!

GOING FOR A TOUCHDOWN

SLIDING DOWN A SLIDING BOARD

Walking

C'MON! I'LL WALK YOU THROUGH SOME WALKING POSES. THEY'RE IMPORTANT TO LEARN BECAUSE THEY CAN SAY A LOT ABOUT THE MOOD OF YOUR CHARACTERS.

THIS SKETCH OF ME LEANING BACK WITH MY HAND IN MY POCKET REFLECTS THAT I AM IN NO HURRY AND JUST OUT FOR A LEISURELY WALK.

THIS POSE SAYS THAT HE IS ON HIS WAY TO SOMEWHERE IMPORTANT. NOTICE THAT HE IS LEANING FORWARD AND SWINGING HIS ARMS.

Dance Walk

Toe pointed up

Head leaning back

DON'T FORGET THE CARTOON EFFECTS AND ACCESSORIES

Sad walk

Short steps

Body leaning forward, head down, and hands in pocket

Confident walk

He's on his way to success

Go to Re-Tooner™

BOARDS #31, #32, AND #33 AND TAKE YOUR MARKER FOR A WALK.

Running

A CARTOONIST MUST LEARN HOW TO DRAW A FEW GOOD RUNNING POSES.

THIS RUNNER LOOKS LIKE HE'S SCARED AND IS RUNNING AWAY FROM SOMETHING. YOU COULD CHANGE THE WHOLE EFFECT BY SIMPLY CHANGING HIS FACIAL EXPRESSION.

HERE IS AN EXAMPLE OF AN EXAGGERATED RUNNING POSE . . .

. . . THAT CAN ONLY BE DONE IN A CARTOON.

Trotting

NOT ACTUALLY A FULL RUN, BUT SHE LOOKS AS IF SHE'S MOVING ALONG QUICKLY.

Sports & Action

NOTICE HOW THESE COMPLETE CARTOONS
START OUT AS SIMPLE SKETCHES WITH BASIC SHAPES.

Skateboarding

Tennis

NOTICE HOW THIS CHARACTER IS
LEANING BACK TO ADD THE FEELING OF STRAINING.

Rowing

Volleyball

Here's a cool trick!

SEE HOW JUST BY CHANGING THE PROPS AND
CLOTHING THE SAME RUNNING POSE CAN FIT FOR ALL THESE SPORTS.

Football

Tennis

Running

Basketball

Boxing

YOU CAN SQUEEZE OUT AN EXTRA
BIT OF HUMOR JUST BY HAVING HIS
LEGS IN THIS POSTION.

Hockey player

DON'T FORGET THOSE CARTOON EFFECTS & ACCESSORIES!

Body Language

BODY LANGUAGE IS AN EXTENSION OF FACIAL EXPRESSIONS. IT HELPS TO FURTHER ILLUSTRATE THE EMOTION THAT YOU WANT YOUR CHARACTER TO CONVEY.

Hopping mad

IT'S TRUE WE NEVER SEE ANYONE ACTUALLY HOPPING MAD . . . BUT HEY, THIS IS CARTOON WORLD!

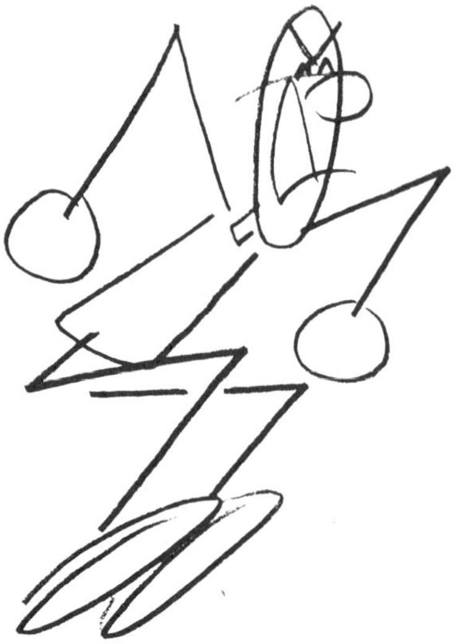

Scolding

THIS GUY IS TELLING HIS DOG THAT HE IS ANGRY WITH SOMETHING THE POOCH DID . . . AND HIS BODY LANGUAGE SHOWS IT. POOR DOG!

In Love

ANOTHER EXAMPLE OF WHAT CAN ONLY BE DONE IN A CARTOON.
I MEAN, PEOPLE DON'T REALLY FLOAT ON AIR WHEN THEY'RE IN LOVE . . . DO THEY?

Animals

THE KEY TO DRAWING CARTOON ANIMALS IS TO "SIMPLIFY" THE "REALISTIC" FEATURES. AS YOU CAN SEE FROM THE "CARTOONIFIED" GIRAFFE BELOW, I HAVE KEPT THE GENERAL SHAPE OF THE REALISTIC ANIMAL BUT HAVE "STYLIZED" IT A BIT BY SMOOTHING OUT THE LUMPS AND BUMPS.

Realistic

Cartoonified

A sea lion

IT ALL BEGINS WITH THIS BENT HOT-DOG SHAPE.

Camel

A CAMEL WITH TWO HUMPS IS A "BACTERINE" CAMEL.

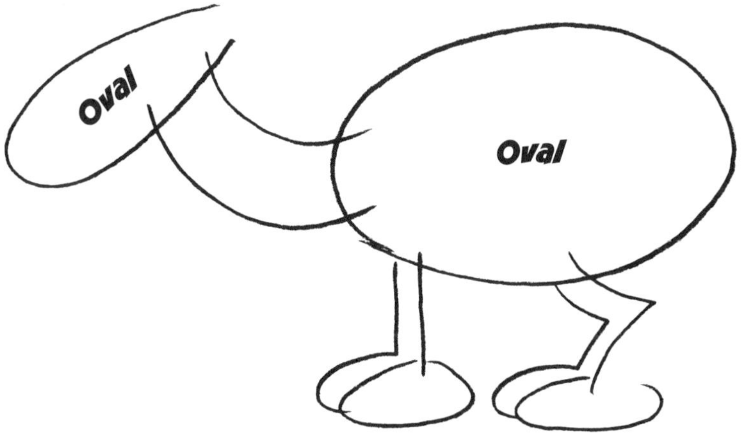

Some basic shapes

ADD ON EYES, NOSE, MOUTH, EARS, AND TAIL. INDICATE THE TWO HUMPS WITH A LOOSE WAVY LINE.

ONCE YOU HAVE "INKED IN" YOUR SKETCH, ADD SOME HAIR.

Dog Running

1. LAY OUT THE BASIC BODY AND HEAD WITH OVALS AND CIRCLES.

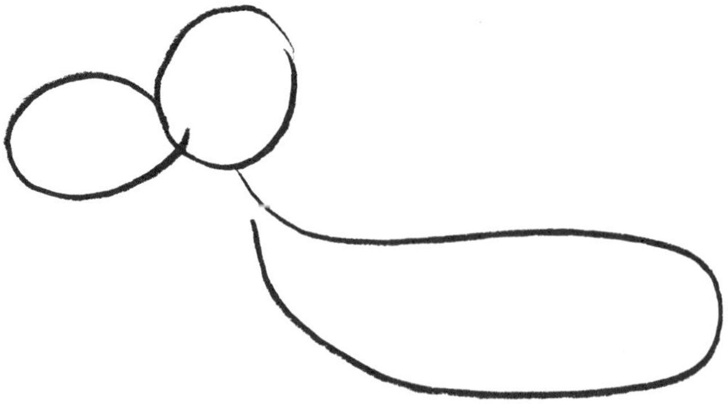

2. ADD NOSE AND EARS, AND SET THE POSITIONING OF THE LEGS.

3. THICKEN UP THE LEGS AND ADD SOME DETAIL.

4. GO OVER THE ENTIRE DRAWING MAKING ONE DEFINITE CARTOON-STYLE BLACK LINE, AND ERASE THE PENCIL.

FROM A BONE TO AN ANIMAL THAT LOVES THEM

Dog

Horse

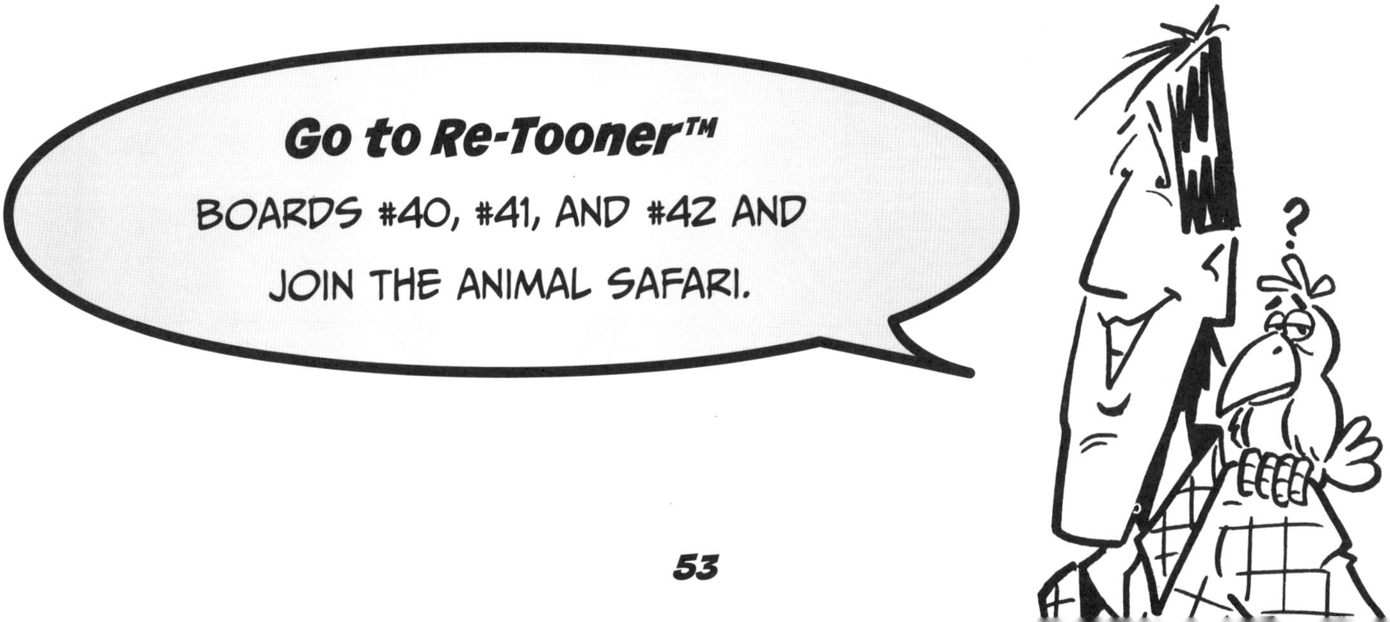

Doodle Tricks

TURNING LETTERS, NUMBERS, AND WORDS INTO FINISHED CARTOONS IS FUN TO DO—AND FUN FOR FRIENDS TO WATCH! IT ALSO HELPS YOU TO DEVELOP A KEEN EYE FOR CREATING CARTOONS.

Alphabetoons

HERE ARE JUST SOME EXAMPLES OF WHAT CAN BE DONE WITH THE LETTERS IN THE ALPHABET.

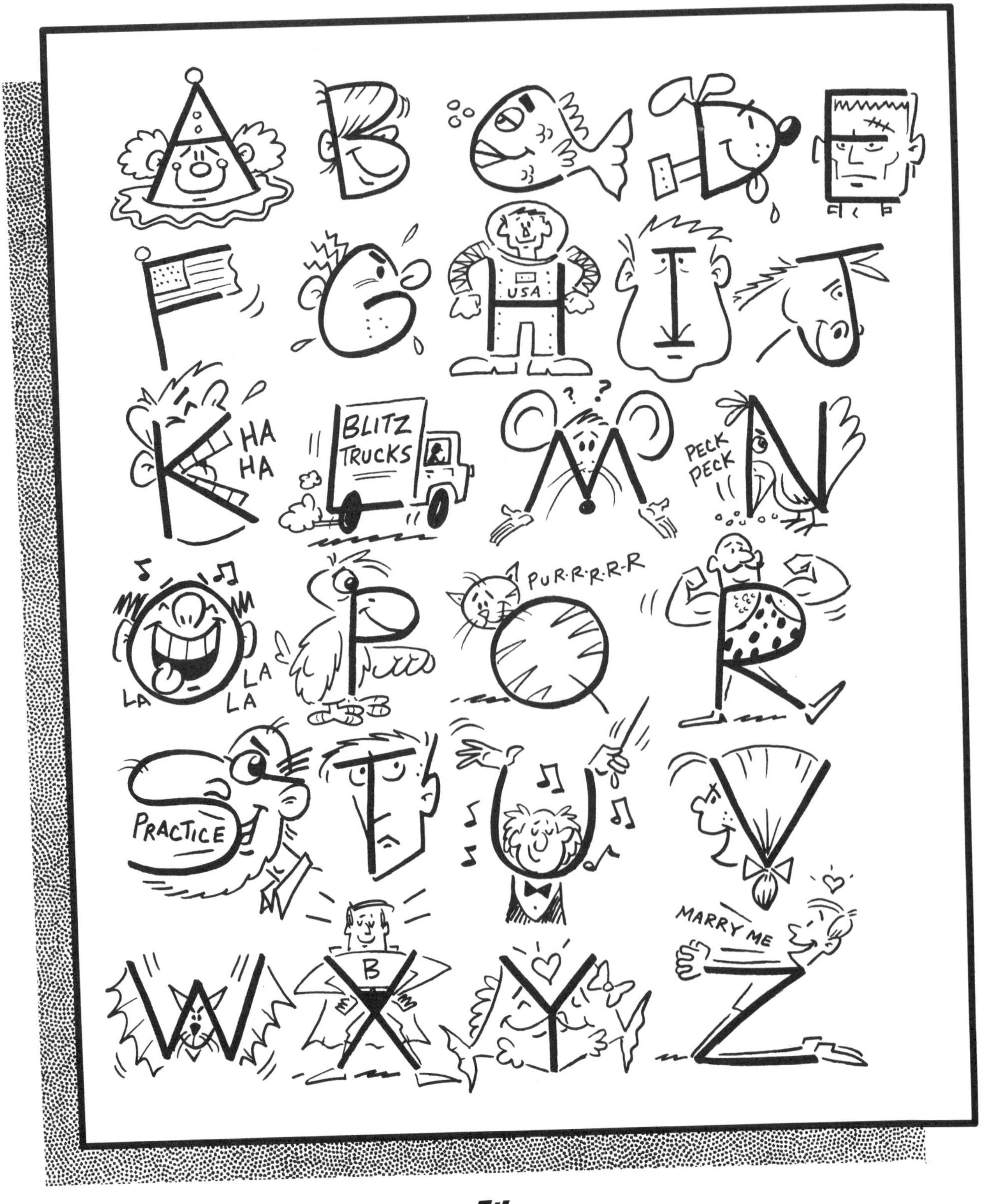

Numbertoons

HERE ARE SOME FINISHED CARTOONS THAT STARTED OUT AS NUMBERS.

Wordtoons

TRY CREATING A CARTOON FROM A THREE-LETTER WORD.

THE WORD "PAL" TURNS INTO A BOY AND HIS PAL!

Go to Re-Tooner™

BOARDS #43 TO #50 AND LEARN HOW TO AMAZE YOUR FRIENDS WITH DOODLE TRICKS. BY THE WAY, DID YOU NOTICE MY NOSE AND EYE WERE CREATED FROM THE NUMBER "2"?

INSPIRATION
FOR CARTOONING IDEAS IS
EVERYWHERE—JUST LOOK AROUND! I
HOPE MY *ULTIMATE CARTOONING KIT*
HAS HELPED YOU BECOME A BETTER
CARTOONIST. THANKS . . . AND
KEEP ON CARTOONING!